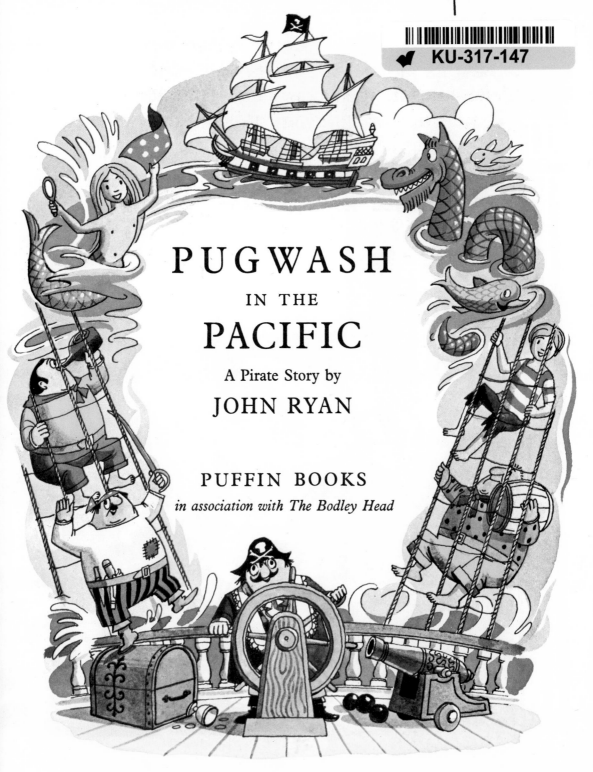

PUGWASH
IN THE
PACIFIC

A Pirate Story by
JOHN RYAN

PUFFIN BOOKS
in association with The Bodley Head

"It's an absolute disgrace, Admiral," said the Prime Minister. "This pirate rascal Pugwash must be captured at all cost! Take a squadron of ships and search the Seven Seas; find the *Black Pig*, catch its Captain and bring him back alive."

Admiral Sir Splycemeigh Mayne-
brace, Commander in Chief of the
British Navy, stood to attention and
saluted.

"Shiver me timbers, Prime Minister,"
he said. "You've chosen the very man
for the job. I'll capture the varmint. Just
leave it to me!"

On a sunny island, far away in the Pacific Ocean, Captain Pugwash was resting happily. It was some weeks after the meeting between the Prime Minister and the Admiral and the Captain was quite unaware of the fearful fate which was bearing down on him. He had had a very good year. The beach was piled high with all the treasure he had stolen from ships smaller and weaker than his own. The sky was blue, the sea was warm and the Captain and his crew were having a lovely time.

Some were having
a barbecue on
the yellow sand

and others were
playing in the
blue-green sea.

Suddenly Tom the cabin boy came running out of the jungle.

"Cap'n, Cap'n!" he cried. "Terrible news! The British Navy . . . they're after you!"

"How-how do you know?" gasped Pugwash.

"From one of the natives on the other side of the island," answered Tom. "The Navy are searching the whole coast; they could be here any minute!"

There was panic amongst the pirates. Some of them
got dressed so as to be able to run away and others got
undressed in case they had to swim for it.

Then the Mate, who was watching the horizon, called out, "A sail, Cap'n, a ship! It's the Navy, that's what it is!"

"Jumping Jellyfish!" exclaimed the Captain. "Take cover, me hearties!" and he and all the pirates fled as fast as they could into the undergrowth. In fact they ran so fast that they left all the treasure behind, and the Captain's hat blew off

and landed on top of the treasure chest. Only Tom stayed behind because he was braver than the others.

While Pugwash and the crew were doing their best to make themselves invisible in the jungle,

Tom looked out to sea
and saw that the ship
which was approaching
was not a naval vessel
at all. It was another
pirate ship and it
belonged to Cut-throat
Jake, the Captain's
worst enemy and the most
wicked buccaneer afloat.

Jake, surrounded by his villainous crew, was inspecting the beach through his telescope.

"Ya-hah-hah-hah!" he growled greedily. "That's a sight for sore eyes, boys! A cosy beach, a pile o' treasure and . . . yes . . . I'd know that *hat*, anywhere!"

"It belongs to that old scallywag Pugwash, fled away at the sight of us! Let's go ashore, me handsomes. We could do with a sunny seaside holiday."

So Jake and his men scrambled into their longboat and rowed towards the shore. They left their ship, which was called *Flying Dustman*, at anchor.

Soon they were happily sunbathing on the beach just as Pugwash and his crew had done earlier. Jake put on the Captain's hat as a trophy and he ordered his men to bury the treasure in the sand, because that is what sensible pirates usually do.

All this time, Tom was keeping an eye on them from the edge of the jungle. As he watched he saw something else, which Jake had not noticed.

The British Naval Squadron was sailing round the island towards them! Tom had an idea, and he ran to where Pugwash and the others were hiding. "Stay here," he told them. "Don't come out *whatever* happens!" That was easy; the Captain was far too frightened even to take his head out of the bushes.

Tom slipped back to the beach, past Jake and his band who were all fast asleep by now, and swam out to Jake's ship. On board he found some black paint and some white paint and a paint brush. He climbed down the stern of the pirates' ship,

painted out *Flying Dustman* and put *Black Pig* instead. Then Tom swam back to the island.

Meanwhile the British Naval Squadron was getting closer. On board his flagship, Admiral Sir Splycemeigh Maynebrace paced up and down impatiently. For weeks now he had been relentlessly scouring the high seas, with never a sign of Pugwash.

As they rounded the next point, there was a cry from the look-out. "Ship ahoy! Ship at anchor on the starboard bow!"

The Admiral seized his telescope. "And *what* a ship by thunder!" he cried.

"Gentlemen, our search is at an end. That ship is the *Black Pig*, with the Jolly Roger at the mast-head . . . and on the beach nearby—yes—the infamous Pugwash himself!"

"Heavily disguised, of course, but I'd know that *hat* anywhere! And his crew are all there, too. Stand by to sink the ship and put a landing party ashore to arrest the ruffians!"

A few minutes later a broadside of heavy naval guns
shattered Cut-throat Jake's ship from stem to stern,
blowing up the powder magazine as it did so. And, at
the same moment a landing party of sailors rushed

upon the sleeping pirates on the beach and took every
one of them prisoner. They carried them struggling
hopelessly back to the flagship . . .

where the Admiral was waiting in triumph.

"Horatio Pugwash, I arrest you in the King's name," said he.

"Pugwash?—Pugwash?—I ain't no such person, Admiral," spluttered Jake.
"Rubbish, man!" roared the Admiral. "Think you can deceive me with a great black beard and an eye-patch? I know a ruffian when I see one. Put him in irons!"

Back in London there was great rejoicing at the news of the capture of the notorious pirate Pugwash. The church bells rang, there was a firework display and the crowds cheered and cheered.

There was a new Prime Minister and he gave a very grand party for Admiral Sir Splycemeigh Mayne-brace. "Well done, Splycemeigh," he said. "They'll probably make you a Duke for this!"

And Cut-throat Jake and his crew were thrown into a deep dank dungeon to await trial for the crimes of Pugwash.

But back on that distant Pacific Island, the real Captain Pugwash had long since dug up his treasure *and* found himself a new hat.

The sky was blue, the sea was warm and life went on lazily and peacefully just as it had before.

"I sometimes wonder," said the Captain, "what happened to that Cut-throat Jake fellow. We don't seem to see very much of him these days."

Tom the cabin boy heard the Captain and smiled. "It's hardly surprising," he thought, but he went on mixing a large bowl of tropical fruit salad for the pirates' supper, and said nothing.